What's wrong with Patti?

The late bell rang, and math class began. Ms. Chipley opened Mrs. Mead's grade book and picked the names of four kids to work out some of the homework problems on the blackboard. Patti was one of the kids she called on.

Patti strolled slowly up to the board, carefully picked up a piece of chalk, and proceeded to do the problem *wrong*! I couldn't believe it, and neither could anybody else in the room.

In science Patti couldn't seem to remember the simplest facts about circulation, like whether the veins pump blood *to* or *from* the heart. It was incredible!

By the time the lunch bell rang, Ms. Chipley was definitely starting to look worried.

Look for these and other books
in the Sleepover Friends Series:

The Trouble with Patti

Susan Saunders

AN
APPLE
PAPERBACK

SCHOLASTIC INC.
New York Toronto London Auckland Sydney

ISBN 0-590-42818-7

12 11 10 9 8 7 6 5 4 3 2 1   0 1 2 3 4 5/9

Printed in the U.S.A.   28

First Scholastic printing, March 1990

The Trouble with Patti

Chapter
1

"I'm probably learning more about science in ten minutes in your kitchen than I will in ten weeks at Riverhurst Elementary!" Kate Beekman murmured to Patti Jenkins.

"Your Uncle Nick makes it a thousand times more fun than Dr. Know," Stephanie Green added in a low voice. Dr. Know has one of those science programs for kids — it's in reruns on Channel 6. "And he's a lot cuter."

Patti's Uncle Nick is definitely cute. He has blondish-brown hair that waves a little in front, a thick mustache, and nice, twinkly blue-gray eyes behind wire-rimmed glasses. "He seems cheerful enough, too," I whispered to Patti — I'm Lauren Hunter.

1

"Maybe right now," Patti whispered back. "But since yesterday he's totally destroyed a lamp and Mom's favorite spider plant! Tell you more when we get upstairs."

Kate, Stephanie, Patti, and I were hanging out in Patti's kitchen, along with her little brother, Horace, watching her uncle Nick Pollard do scientific experiments. He was using everyday household stuff — vinegar and salt and pepper and baking soda — just like Dr. Know, only better.

We'd already seen the bouncing egg trick. Pretty cool — a hard-boiled egg *in its shell*, bouncing across the tile floor! The secret is to soak the egg in vinegar for a day. Vinegar's an acid, and it eats into the hard shell and makes it soft.

Then Uncle Nick showed us how to make a magnifier out of a drop of water on a clear glass plate. A water drop is naturally round, and its curved shape magnifies everything you look at, just like a lens. We read the small print of a cereal box with it: "If you are not entirely satisfied with the quality of this product . . ."

Next Horace did Uncle Nick's Super Separating Salt and Pepper Trick. First you mix a spoonful of salt and a spoonful of pepper together in a glass. That's easy enough, but what do you do if you want to separate them again? Pick out the pepper with tweezers, a flake at a time? It would take *forever*. So . . . you just fill the glass with water, and bingo! All the pepper floats to the top, and all the salt sinks to the bottom. That's because pepper is lighter than water, and salt is heavier.

Just then we were gathered around the kitchen table watching Uncle Nick pour milk into a small bowl. "That's plenty," he said when the bowl was about a quarter full. "Now, what are your favorite colors?"

"Blue," I answered. I like blue because it goes with practically everything.

"Red!" said Stephanie.

"Yellow?" Patti replied.

"Green," Kate said firmly.

"I like brown!" Horace piped up. *Brown*?! Well, he is only six years old.

"I'm afraid we don't have any brown food coloring, sport," Uncle Nick said. "We have all the other colors, though. So we add one small drop of each . . ." He carefully dripped a single dot of blue, then red, yellow, and green food coloring into the middle of the bowl of milk. The little circles of color just sat on the surface of the milk, hardly spreading out at all.

"And then the magic ingredient!" Uncle Nick picked up the plastic bottle of dishwashing liquid next to the sink. He squirted a stream of detergent high up on the side of the bowl. It flowed down the side and slipped into the milk without even jiggling it. The colored dots didn't so much as bobble!

"And now, watch . . ." Uncle Nick said, peering at the milk. "Here it comes. . . ." A couple of seconds later, the dots absolutely exploded into tiny fountains and whirlpools of color! It was fabulous!

"Wow!" Horace exclaimed. "Why did it do that?"

"Well, you know how everything in the world is made up of microscopic molecules?" Uncle Nick asked.

"Sure," Horace answered offhandedly. "And molecules are made up of atoms!" He may be only six, but the kid's practically a genius when it comes to science.

"We'll just focus on the molecules right now," Uncle Nick told him. "And the fact that one part of each soap molecule loves water, and one part hates water. Like maybe some of you *hate* getting your head wet when you're swimming?"

"Exactly!" Stephanie said. She has naturally

curly hair that turns into major frizzies if she even *thinks* about water.

"Well, soap molecules are the same way," Uncle Nick continued. "Milk has a lot of water in it. And as soon as the soap molecules touch it, they rearrange themselves so that the parts that love water face into the milk, while the parts that hate water face into the air. In order for the molecules to manage that, they have to spread out across the surface of the milk. . . ."

"And the spreading out of the molecules is what moves the food coloring around!" Patti said. "We can't actually *see* the molecules doing it — they're too small — but we can see what happens to the top of the milk *while* they're doing it."

"Correct-o!" Uncle Nick agreed.

The food coloring eventually stopped swirling around. Now the milk in the bowl looked like a three-year-old's finger-painting with all the colors mushed together. "Show's over," Uncle Nick said, picking up the bowl. "Dump this in the sink, okay, Horace?"

"Thanks," Stephanie said. "That was really neat!"

"And thank you for being such a great audience!" Uncle Nick bowed just a little. "Horace and

I were getting tired of the same old faces — his and mine."

"Hey, want to see a volcano, Lauren?" Horace said with a big grin. He was standing in front of the sink, holding a tall glass of clear liquid in one hand and a box of baking soda in the other.

"No!" Patti yelped before I could answer. She made a grab for Horace, but she wasn't quite fast enough to stop him from dumping a heap of baking soda into the glass.

Suddenly the clear liquid churned up into a thick, bubbling foam that erupted over the rim of the glass, flowed across his hand, and ran down his arm onto the floor!

"Yipes!" said Kate.

"Good work, Horace," Patti said grimly. She snatched the foaming glass and poured it into the sink.

"I did it right, didn't I, Uncle Nick?" Horace said, squeezing suds out of his shirtsleeve.

"I couldn't have done it better myself," Uncle Nick said, laughing as he reached for a sponge.

"What was that stuff?" I asked, half expecting it to fizz up again.

"Just vinegar, soap, and baking soda in water," Uncle Nick said, mopping at the bubbles on the floor.

"Together the vinegar and baking soda form a gas that makes the soap bubble up. Great stuff, huh?"

Patti glanced around the kitchen. Almost every surface was covered with plates, bowls, bottles, and jars that Uncle Nick and Horace had used in some experiment or other. It looked like the mad scientist's laboratory in one of those old sci-fi films Kate's always watching, like *Professor X and the Doomsday Potion*.

Patti sighed. "I guess we'd better get started cleaning up this mess," she said to her uncle.

"Oh, no — Horace and I will take care of it," Uncle Nick told her. "You ladies just collect your snacks and go right ahead with your sleepover."

Besides being in the same class at school and spending most of our free time together, Patti, Kate, Stephanie, and I take turns having sleepovers at one another's houses on Fridays. That Friday night it happened to be Patti's turn.

"Well . . . okay," Patti said a little doubtfully. "But if you need any help . . ."

Uncle Nick shook his head. "Don't worry about a thing. The guys can handle it." He grinned at Horace.

Patti shrugged. "All right . . . Kate, could you put some ice in glasses while I microwave the egg rolls?'' She reached into the freezer. ''Oh, and Lauren, why don't you pull the big white tray out of the closet. There's a bag of cheddar cheese popcorn in the basket at the end of the counter.''

I'm getting to know my way around Patti's and Stephanie's kitchens almost as well as I do my own. Or Kate's. Kate and I have been in and out of each other's houses since we were babies. We're practically next-door neighbors on Pine Street, so we started playing together while we were still in diapers. By kindergarten, we were best friends. That's when the sleepovers started. Every Friday either I would sleep over at the Beekmans', or Kate would spend the night at my house. It got to be such a regular thing that Kate's dad named us the Sleepover Twins.

Not that we were very much alike, even way back then. I was always taller than Kate. Also, I have dark hair, while she's short and blonde. Kate's sensible; I sometimes let my imagination run away with me. I like sports; Kate prefers a shady seat on the sidelines. Still, for all our differences, we hardly ever have a serious disagreement.

At our early sleepovers, we played Dress-Up and Let's Pretend. We filled the ice-cube trays with cherry Kool-Aid, or melted s'mores all over the toaster oven and called it "cooking."

As we got older, Kate perfected her recipe for marshmallow super-fudge, and I invented my own special dip made of onion soup, olives, bacon bits, and sour cream. It goes great with everything from carrot sticks to barbecue potato chips. We also put in thousands of hours in front of our TV sets, watching movies: black-and-white, color, old, new, musicals, silents, you name it. Kate wants to be a movie director someday so she'll watch just about anything!

When we weren't glued to the TV, we spied on my older brother, Roger, and his friends, or thought up ways to keep Kate's little sister, Melissa, from spying on *us*. We made up our own Mad Libs and started playing Truth or Dare. And in all that time, we never had a major argument . . . until Stephanie Green came to town last year.

The Greens moved to Riverhurst from the city, into a house at the far end of Pine Street. Stephanie and I got to know each other because we were both in 4A, Mr. Civello's class.

Stephanie knew tons about fashion. In the fourth grade, she already had her own style of dressing worked out, like almost always wearing black, red, and white, which looks great with her dark hair. Stephanie was funny. She told great stories about life in the city, and she knew most of the latest dances. I thought she was terrific, and I wanted Kate to get to know her, too. So I invited Stephanie to a Friday sleepover at my house.

Talk about an experiment that didn't work out! Kate thought Stephanie was an airhead who only cared about shopping. Stephanie thought Kate was a stuffy know-it-all. The sleepover was an experience neither of them wanted to repeat, *ever!*

But I don't give up that easily. Since Stephanie lives on Pine Street like Kate and me, it was only natural that we fell into the habit of riding our bikes to school together most mornings. Then I just happened to run into Stephanie at the mall a couple of Saturday afternoons when Kate was with me. We managed to get through that without major problems. A few weeks later Stephanie asked me to a sleepover at her house. I told her I absolutely *had* to bring Kate, since *our* Fridays were a regular thing.

At that sleepover, we ate platters of Mrs. Green's yummy peanut-butter-chocolate-chip cookies. Then we watched three movies in a row on Stephanie's private TV, which definitely softened Kate up a little. Finally, Kate invited Stephanie to a Friday sleepover at the Beekmans'. And the Sleepover Twins slowly became a trio.

Not that Kate and Stephanie suddenly agreed about *everything*, not by a long shot. Half the time I'd end up feeling like a referee! Which is only one of the reasons I was glad when Patti Jenkins turned up in Mrs. Mead's class this fall, along with Kate, Stephanie, and me.

Patti's from the city, too. She and Stephanie even went to the same school for a couple of years. But Patti's as quiet and shy as Stephanie is bubbly and outgoing. Patti's also one of the smartest kids at Riverhurst Elementary, as well as one of the nicest. And she's taller than I am, which is another plus. Stephanie's as short as Kate, and I was tired of being the giant of the group.

Stephanie wanted Patti to be part of our gang, and both Kate and I liked her right away. So school had barely started this year, and presto! There were *four* Sleepover Friends!

Patti was piling plates and bowls onto the tray, along with the egg rolls and drinks. "Stephanie, could you bring the paper napkins and a spoon for the dip?" she asked. Kate picked up a big bowl of Patti's Alaska dip — tuna, cream cheese, and other good stuff, smoothed out in a blender. I tucked the cheddar cheese popcorn under one arm and a bag of blue corn chips under the other. And the four of us headed for the door.

Patti glanced worriedly over her shoulder toward the kitchen. "I hope nothing goes wrong . . . ," she murmured.

"They'll manage," Stephanie said firmly, giving her a little push.

But we were barely halfway up the stairs when there was a loud *crash* below us!

"Oh, no!" Patti groaned. "Not again."

As we hurried back down, Stephanie whispered to Kate and me, "When did Patti say her parents are getting back?"

Chapter
2

"Whenever it is, it's not soon enough," Kate muttered as we burst into the kitchen. "If Mr. and Mrs. Jenkins could see this, they'd probably faint!"

There was a mound of broken dishes between the table and the counter. Not just broken, but *smashed*, so that the pieces looked like pottery confetti, with a couple of puddles of food-coloring decorating the pile. Horace and Uncle Nick were gazing down at the evidence, their hands behind their backs as though they'd had nothing to do with the wreckage. Then they stared up at us with guilty expressions.

"It wasn't my fault!" Horace blurted out.

"No, it was mine," Uncle Nick said. "Actually, it was the bubble soap I mixed up." He'd given us all the recipe earlier: eight tablespoons of detergent, a quart of water, a wire shaped into a circle or square or whatever you like, and you're all set to blow dynamite bubbles. "I guess a little must have spilled on the floor. . . ."

"And my foot slipped on it, and I dropped a few old plates," Horace said crossly.

"I think Uncle Nick's rubbing off on Horace," Stephanie mumbled under her breath.

"I couldn't help it," Horace was saying.

Uncle Nick agreed with his nephew. "That's right. His foot hit the bubble juice. One leg went one way, one went the other, and the dishes crashed against the edge of the sink. We're just lucky Horace didn't get hurt. But don't worry. We've got everything under control now."

Patti didn't seem to think so, though. Once we'd trudged past the second floor and headed up the narrow flight of steps to the attic, Kate asked, "Has Uncle Nick always been sort of . . . klutzy?"

Patti shrugged. "A little," she replied gloomily. "But it's gotten *much* worse since the Maureen Matson mess!"

Maureen Matson used to be Uncle Nick's girlfriend — until a few weeks ago.

Uncle Nick had taken time off from his job in France to come back to the United States to get engaged to her. But he'd no sooner arrived in Chicago than Maureen had turned him down flat. She had said she didn't want to move to Europe. And that was how Uncle Nick ended up spending his vacation at the Jenkinses'.

"He can't seem to concentrate on *anything*, not even on his own two feet," Patti said. She stopped outside the door to the attic and frowned. "About half the time, he's absentmindedly dropping or tripping over stuff. Last night he even stepped on his sandwich. Or else he'll just sit in the living room in the dark, watching Dr. Know reruns with the sound turned off.

"I'm not sure which is worse — having Uncle Nick wrecking the place, or parking himself somewhere, like a totally depressed *lump*."

Patti pushed open the attic door, switched on the single overhead light, and Kate, Stephanie, and I followed her inside.

The Jenkinses' attic is huge. It's an open space running across the whole top of the house, with crisscrossing rafters that come to a point in the center, and little round windows in each wall that look like portholes. It's great for sleepovers, because we can make as much noise as we like without disturbing anybody.

Patti closed the door behind us and went on, "My mom is really going to be upset about those dishes, too. She's had that blue bowl since she and my dad got married, and the plate with yellow flowers on it was a present from her grandmother!"

She set the tray down on an old rug spread out on the floor, and collapsed beside it. "And when Uncle Nick tries to *fix* things it's even worse! We've had a leak in the faucet in the bathroom for a few days. Nothing drastic, a couple of drops of water in the sink now and then. This afternoon, though, Uncle Nick decided to repair it. He ended up snapping a pipe and squirting water all over the place! We had to call an emergency plumber, and it took us half an hour to mop up!" She shook her head and sighed again.

Stephanie, Kate, and I sat down on the rug, too. Patti handed each of us a giant glass of Cherry Coke, and I tore open the bag of blue corn chips. "How does Uncle Nick know so much about science?" I asked her. "I thought he was an engineer."

"Chemical engineer," Patti said. "You know — chemistry?"

"So being good at science runs in the family," Kate said.

Patti shrugged and changed the subject. "Anybody want some dip?'' Talking about how smart she is makes her uncomfortable.

But, as I said, Patti happens to be one of the smartest kids at Riverhurst Elementary. She's good at everything having to do with school, but she's especially good at science. Patti belongs to a club called the Quarks, for kids who are science whizzes. It's sponsored partly by Riverhurst Elementary and partly by the university.

Not that Patti ever brags about her brains or anything. And Mrs. Mead, our teacher, is cool about it, too. She doesn't embarrass the kids who do badly by calling attention to them during class. And she doesn't make the really smart kids feel funny by holding them up as examples, either.

After we'd dug into the dip with blue corn chips, and we'd each snagged an egg roll or two, I asked, ''So, how long *will* your parents be gone, Patti?''

''Seven more days,'' she said. ''The conference is over on Wednesday, and then they're going to visit some friends in Washington.'' Both of Patti's parents are history professors at the university. Mr. Jenkins teaches modern history, and Mrs. Jenkins specializes in stuff that was going on two thousand years ago. ''By the time they get back, Uncle Nick will have completely destroyed the house!''

"Not necessarily," Stephanie said, balancing a glob of dip on a corn chip. "It seems to me there's an easy way to keep that from happening."

"Right, do not pass Go, do not collect two hundred dollars, and send Uncle Nick straight back to Europe," Kate said with a grin. "But somehow I don't think Mr. and Mrs. Jenkins would be too happy about Patti and Horace spending a week on their own."

"Ha, ha," Stephanie said, making a face at her. "I'm serious!"

"What? You have a plan?" I asked. Stephanie's always coming up with crazy schemes that actually work out sometimes.

"Sure. We find Uncle Nick a new girlfriend, right here in Riverhurst," Stephanie said breezily. "His mind snaps back to normal, and the rest of Mrs. Jenkins' dishes, lamps, plants, pipes, and sandwiches stay in one piece."

"A girlfriend?" Patti said uncertainly. She was undoubtedly remembering all of Stephanie's plans that *haven't* worked out.

"Isn't it a little too soon for a new girlfriend?" I said. "I mean, just last week the man was almost engaged."

"We could find him someone to go out with at least," Stephanie said.

"How old is Uncle Nick?" Kate asked Patti.

"Twenty-eight last October," Patti replied.

"He's a little out of our age group, don't you think?" Kate said to Stephanie. "I mean, it's not exactly the same thing as going up to Jane Sykes and saying, 'Mark Freedman likes you; do you want to meet him at the Pizza Palace on Saturday?'" Jane Sykes and Mark Freedman are both kids in 5B, our class at Riverhurst Elementary.

Patti nodded. "I feel kind of weird even talking about this," she said. "If Uncle Nick knew I'd told you about his problems, he might be really — "

"Why would he ever have to know? I'm not suggesting we announce, 'Uncle Nick, we feel so sorry for you because you got dumped that we've decided to fix you up.'" Stephanie waved her egg roll in the air to make a point. "If we play our cards right, he'll think it's all his idea."

"And just how are we going to manage that?" Kate asked, raising an eyebrow.

"First we have to think of women in the *right age group*," Stephanie replied, with a nod to Kate. "And then we figure out which ones have something in common with Uncle Nick, and eliminate the others.''

"Yeah — I read an article in *Teen Topics* about those computer-dating services,'' I said. "You list your likes and dislikes, your hobbies, and your goals. Then they feed them into the computer, and come up with the people who match you the closest. Only in this case, *we*'d be the computer!'' I was starting to get into it!

"Who do we know who's in her middle or late twenties, who's not married, or even engaged?'' Stephanie said. "Come on, Kate — think of someone! You and Lauren have lived here a lot longer than Patti and I have, and Uncle Nick needs our help.''

Kate glanced at Patti, who was still trying to make up her mind whether or not this was a good idea. When Patti finally shrugged her shoulders, Kate said, "Okay, okay. What about Lucy Wilder?''

"Excellent,'' Stephanie exclaimed, drumming her feet on the floor excitedly. Lucy Wilder is the new manager at Just Juniors at the mall, which is a store that sells great kids' clothes. "She's nice, she's cute-looking, she's a fabulous dresser, and she has lots of personality. Uncle Nick's bound to like her; everybody does. And I'm sure she'll like him.

"I can see it all now," Stephanie continued dreamily. "We'll be the bridesmaids at their wedding, in matching outfits from the shop, and then we'll all get store discounts, because Lucy will be in the family!"

"Ho-o-old on!" Kate said, waving her hand to slow Stephanie down. "Before we start picking out a new wardrobe, what makes Uncle Nick and Lucy right for each other? We don't know a thing about her."

"What about Uncle Nick?" I said to Patti. "What are his hobbies? His likes and dislikes?"

Patti frowned thoughtfully. "I guess his main hobby is Oddjob." Oddjob is a small, metal robot that Uncle Nick put together in his spare time. He has treads for feet, two arms that look like Slinkys, and a little round head with dish-shaped antennas for ears. "He's been working on Oddjob in the basement since he got here."

I personally think Oddjob is neat. Uncle Nick left the robot at the Jenkinses' when he went to Europe, and we've messed around with him a few times. But I wasn't sure if robots were Lucy Wilder's style. . . .

I guess Stephanie wasn't sure either, because she said, "I like Oddjob myself, but fooling around with

21

robots could strike some people as sort of geeky, don't you think? Does Uncle Nick have any other hobbies?"

"Well . . . he takes lots of pictures," Patti said.

"Photography's good," Stephanie said. "What about likes and dislikes?"

"He likes music," Patti replied.

"Great! So does Lucy," I said. Lucy always has the stereo on full-blast at the store, playing nonstop heavy metal.

"I'm not sure he likes *that* kind of music," Patti said doubtfully. "Uncle Nick mostly listens to golden oldies. And how are we ever going to get them together, anyway? I don't know, guys. This could turn out to be awfully complicated. Maybe we should just forget — "

She was interrupted by a loud knock on the attic door. "Who is it?" Patti said.

"Let us in!" It was Horace and Uncle Nick. "We've got something to show you!"

Chapter
3

Patti scrambled to her feet and opened the attic door. Horace was standing on the next to the last step, holding a big, gray rubber bucket. Uncle Nick was waiting on the step below Horace, and he was carrying Oddjob.

"Since this is the biggest room in the house, we thought it would be the best place to demonstrate Oddjob's latest moves," Uncle Nick said. He and Horace walked to the center of the room. Horace put down the gray bucket, and Uncle Nick set Oddjob down on his treads. "Okay, Oddjob, let's show 'em what we've learned. Ready?"

There was a whole series of whirs and clicks as Oddjob warmed up. Finally the robot replied in his crackly voice, "Read-dy, Nick."

Uncle Nick took a curved wire out of his shirt pocket and gave it to Oddjob. Oddjob gripped the wire tightly in one of his three-fingered hands. Uncle Nick nudged the gray bucket against the robot's leg, and Oddjob bent over to pick it up with his other hand. He dipped the wire into the bucket and pulled it out dripping with Uncle Nick's special bubble recipe. Then he held the wire up over his head. A few clickety-clicks and the robot suddenly sped smoothly across the attic floor with a string of bubbles stretching out behind him!

The bubbles drifted toward the pointed ceiling, sparkling in the light. Oddjob dipped the wire into the bucket again. With a high-pitched whir that sounded almost like *wheee*, he spun around and around on his treads, surrounding himself with big, shiny bubbles.

"Maybe it's not as useful as vacuuming and dusting," Uncle Nick said (he originally designed the robot to do odd jobs around the house), "but it's a lot more fun."

Patti and Kate clapped, and I said, "It sure *looks* like fun!"

"I'd like to try it!" Stephanie said.

"Great! I've got plenty of wires for everybody!" Uncle Nick said.

So the four of us, plus Uncle Nick and Horace, all dipped into Oddjob's bubble bucket. Then we spun ourselves around or raced across the attic floor holding three or four wires at a time. We blew double bubbles, monster bubbles, and zillions of tiny bubbles with pieces of plastic strawberry baskets. Before long, the attic was absolutely *filled* with bubbles of all sizes. It was like being caught inside a giant bubble machine!

"See? Uncle Nick's having a great time," Kate murmured to me as we watched him doing jumping-jacks with two bubble wires in each hand. "I think he's perfectly capable of working out his problems without us butting in."

But she spoke just a little too soon. The very next time Uncle Nick hurried toward Oddjob and the bubble bucket, he caught his sneaker in the fringe of the old rug. He tried to keep his balance by steadying himself on Oddjob, but as Uncle Nick lurched toward him, the robot spun out of the way.

Squawking noisily, Oddjob threw his slinky arms high in the air, and took off across the attic. The bubble mixture went splashing out of the bucket. It scored a direct hit on Stephanie, who'd taken a break and was sitting on the rug munching on a handful of cheddar cheese popcorn.

"Glub!" Stephanie wiped at the bubble mix running down her face with the sleeve of her red-and-white sweater. "My hair is frizzing!" she wailed. "I can *feel* it!"

"I am *really* sorry," Uncle Nick said, untangling his sneaker from the rug.

"That's all right," Stephanie mumbled. She rubbed her soapy eyes and blinked a few times.

Oddjob was reeling around the far end of the attic with his empty bucket, whirring excitedly. Horace was in hot pursuit, trying to calm him down.

Uncle Nick reached into a back pocket of his jeans for Oddjob's remote control, and switched the robot off with a push of the button. "What about a towel, Stephanie?" he said apologetically. "I'll bring one up. And I'm sure Patti can lend you a dry sweatshirt. . . ."

"It's going to take more than a towel," Stephanie groaned. She tugged at her wet, soapy hair, trying to straighten out the tight curls that were springing up all over her head.

"We'll go downstairs to the bathroom, Uncle Nick," Patti said, glancing at the pool of bubble mix on the floor. To Stephanie she added, "Don't worry. Mom has a brand-new blow dryer."

So Patti, Stephanie, Kate, and I left Uncle Nick

and Horace cleaning up yet another mess, and we trooped downstairs to Patti's parents' bathroom.

Stephanie stuck her head under the shower to get what was left of the bubble mixture off. Then Kate and I sat down on the edge of the tub. Patti held the blow dryer pointed at Stephanie's hair, and Stephanie began to brush her curls straighter.

"What was it you were saying before Uncle Nick showed up in the attic, Patti?" Stephanie said, fixing Patti with an eagle eye in the bathroom mirror. "That we should forget about helping him out?"

"Well . . . uh . . . I guess . . . ," Patti fumbled, not meeting her gaze.

"Kate, too," I announced from the tub. " 'Uncle Nick is perfectly capable of working out his problems without us butting in.' " I quoted Kate exactly.

"Okay, okay, so I was wrong," Kate grumbled.

"Patti?" Stephanie said.

Patti shrugged hopelessly. "Somebody has to do *something*," she agreed. "What if he goes back to his job in this shape?"

"He'll probably destroy half of France," Stephanie muttered. She tugged the brush through the left side of her head, where a handful of curls was kicking up. "So what do we do?" After a pause, she answered herself: "Figure out a way to introduce Uncle Nick to Lucy Wilder as soon as possible!"

"What about tomorrow?" I said. "Lucy's always at Just Juniors on Saturdays."

"Perfect!" Stephanie said, putting her brush down and turning around to face the three of us. "All we have to do is talk him into going to the mall with us. . . ."

"Drag him kicking and screaming into Just Juniors," Kate said, not very enthusiastically.

"And Lucy Wilder will do the rest!" Stephanie finished.

"What if she doesn't?" Kate asked.

"Then we'll have some backups," Stephanie replied matter-of-factly. "Like . . . Miss Emerson, at the Riverhurst Free Library! She's attractive, she's very nice, and she's — "

"Very engaged," Patti interrupted. "Miss Emerson showed me her engagement ring last Sunday when I was working on my Quarks astronomy project."

"What about some of the teachers at Riverhurst Elementary?" Kate suggested. She was getting involved in spite of herself.

"Good idea!" Stephanie said. "Patti, I lent you my *Round-Up* a couple of weeks ago. . . ." The Riverhurst Elementary School *Round-Up* is a little

28

green book that comes out at the end of the school year, with pictures in it of all the classes, students, and teachers.

"It's in my room," Patti said.

"Let's check it out!" Stephanie exclaimed, giving up on her hair for the time being.

We rushed into Patti's room, plopped down on her double bed, and began leafing through last year's *Round-Up*.

"Miss Steinforth, in the first grade?" Patti said, pointing to a teacher at the back of a room filled with smiling kids missing one or more of their front teeth.

"Hmmm . . . that's a possibility," Stephanie said, studying the picture. "She's awfully tall, though."

"Uncle Nick is six-one," Patti told her.

"Let's keep Miss Steinforth in mind," Stephanie said.

"What about Miss Rosen, in third?" Kate asked, tapping a photograph of a small, dark-haired woman with a great smile. "She's Melissa's teacher, and Melissa just loves her. Although that *could* be a bad sign. . . ." We don't call Kate's little sister Melissa the Monster for nothing!

Stephanie shook her head. "No good. I saw Miss Rosen in Charlie's Soda Fountain a couple of weeks ago, holding hands with a really cute guy."

"And Miss Johnson in fourth grade is now Mrs. Lufrano," I said, flipping the page.

"Too bad Mrs. Mead is married," Stephanie mumbled, looking at the picture of last year's 5B. "She'd be perfect."

"Stephanie! Not only is she married, but she already has two children," Kate pointed out.

"I know, I know," Stephanie said, giggling. "Get a load of Bill Bertolas before he grew. He looks about two feet tall here. His feet barely touch the floor."

"Well, he's grown about two feet up and two feet out since then," Kate said. "He's going to be in the Science Bowl, isn't he, Patti?" The Science Bowl is a contest held once a year between teams of kids from Riverhurst Elementary and two nearby schools, Dannerville and Hampton. Each team tries to answer scientific questions, and the team with the most correct answers wins a big gold trophy.

"Yes — Bill and Harriet Mills and Lindsay Vlasak," Patti replied. "They're all in the Quarks."

"And they're all sixth-graders?" I asked, because there are plenty of fourth- and fifth-graders in the Quarks Club, too.

"I guess Mrs. Wainwright thought they'd have

a better chance than younger kids," Patti said. Mrs. Wainwright's the principal at our school, and who's going to argue with *her*?

Kate turned more pages of the *Round-Up*. "Miss Brinkerhoff moved to the city last summer, Miss Larson is now Mrs. Jones . . ." she said, ticking them off with her fingers. "We're running out of teachers!"

"We completely forgot about Ms. Gilberto!" Stephanie had stopped at a picture of a thin young woman with long, dark hair pulled back on the sides.

"Ms. Gilberto?!" Kate, Patti, and I said at the same time. Ms. Gilberto's the art teacher at school, and while she's very nice, she's *awfully* jumpy. The slightest thing upsets her. Just two kids having a friendly argument can practically make her have a nervous breakdown!

"Why not?" said Stephanie. Stephanie's good at art. She's always hanging around the art studio, so she knows Ms. Gilberto better than we do. "She's into photography, like Uncle Nick. I mean, she sponsors the Video Club! And maybe being around him would mellow her out!"

" 'Mellow her out'?" Patti and Kate and I repeated like a chorus. From what we'd seen of Uncle Nick that didn't seem too likely.

"Just think about it," Stephanie said.

31

"While we're thinking, could we go down to the kitchen?" I asked. "I'm starving, and I have a feeling that our snacks in the attic are drowning in bubble juice by now."

"Sure," Patti said. "I know a great experiment we can do with everyday household items. We mix together milk, a raw egg, and some oil in a bowl . . ."

"No more experiments!" Stephanie moaned, pointing to her hair.

". . . add cake mix, and pop it in the micro-wave," Patti finished with a giggle.

"Now, that's my kind of science!" I exclaimed as Kate and Stephanie burst out laughing.

Chapter 4

We didn't have to deal with Uncle Nick or Horace any more that evening. By the time we trooped downstairs to the kitchen for more food, Horace had gone to bed. And Uncle Nick was planted in the den. He was watching TV in the dark, with the sound off.

We didn't want to bother him so we peered cautiously around the door at him. But he didn't even notice we were there. He was staring at the screen with a faraway look in his eyes. "This is a man who is working out his own problems?" Stephanie whispered to Kate. "Give me a break!"

The next morning, Uncle Nick was still down in the dumps, although he tried to hide it. He fiddled with one of the blueberry waffles we'd made for breakfast, pushing it around in the syrup on his plate.

In my book, anyone who doesn't feel like eating a homemade blueberry waffle is definitely in trouble. Finally, to make conversation, he asked us, "Any plans for today?" We all looked at each other. The perfect opening!

"We were thinking about going to the mall this afternoon," Stephanie answered.

"To window-shop," Patti said quickly.

"And maybe stop in for some pizza," I added. "The Pizza Palace has dynamite double-cheese with anchovies."

Uncle Nick perked up a little. "I love pizza," he said, "especially double-cheese with anchovies." We already knew that, because Patti had told us so the night before. Normally we'd rather gag than eat anchovy pizza. But this was all part of our plan to bring Uncle Nick and Lucy Wilder together.

"The only thing is, my bike is broken," Stephanie said in a disappointed voice. That wasn't totally true. Her *old* bike was broken, but her *new* bike was fine.

"Why don't I just drive everybody?" Uncle Nick suggested, which was exactly what we hoped he'd say.

"You mean you'll come to the mall *with* us?" Patti said.

"Why not?" Uncle Nick replied. Then he sighed. Poor guy — how else could we fill those empty hours?

"Great!" Patti smiled at her uncle. "You treat us to pizza . . ."

"And we'll show you all the best stores at the mall!" Stephanie said.

"It's a deal," said Uncle Nick.

The horn honked outside my house at exactly one o'clock. Uncle Nick was driving Mr. Jenkins' van. He was wearing a blue tweed sweater that almost matched his eyes, his hair waved across his forehead, and his blondish mustache was turned up at the ends. He looked terrific!

Patti was sitting in the front seat with Uncle Nick. I climbed into the second seat next to Kate.

"Where's Horace?" I asked.

"He's spending the afternoon with the Reese twins," Patti said.

Even better! It's kind of hard to be cool when there's a little kid around, asking questions and acting up. And we were definitely going to have to be cool to get this to work!

As soon as we'd picked up Stephanie, we drove straight to the mall. We decided to stop in at the

Pizza Palace first, because Patti and Uncle Nick hadn't eaten lunch yet.

No way does the Pizza Palace live up to its name. It's even small for a pizza parlor — just one tiny room with a long counter and six stools along one wall, four video games by the door, and a big, black pizza oven that keeps the whole place pretty hot. Still, they do serve great pizza. Patti, Kate, Stephanie, and I sat down at the counter and placed our order with John, the cook. He looked kind of startled when we asked for double-cheese with *anchovies*, but Uncle Nick didn't notice. He was dropping a quarter into Alien Attackers.

Over the bings and whistles of the video game, Stephanie whispered to Patti, "How's his mood?"

"It's hard to tell," Patti murmured. "He spent most of the morning reading the newspaper."

"Nothing broken around the house?" Kate asked.

"No," said Patti.

"Well, at least that's an improvement," I said.

"I think it's basically just that he didn't move from the couch," Patti replied gloomily.

Then Alien Attackers made a rude noise, meaning the game was over. Patti glanced back at the score on the screen and shook her head. "Only thirty-three thousand four hundred," she said sadly. "He usually makes at least five times that."

"Pie's ready!" John, the cook, announced.

I'm always hungry. Kate and Stephanie have given me all kinds of nicknames because of my appetite, like the Endless Stomach, the Bottomless Pit, or the Hollow Leg. But just looking at those hairy little fish-strips floating on an ocean of melted cheese made me kind of seasick.

I forced myself to eat one slice. Kate, Stephanie, and Patti couldn't manage even that much. Uncle Nick didn't seem to have an appetite, either, especially considering this was supposed to be one of his favorite foods. He only ate two slices and drank half a glass of Dr Pepper.

We did a little better at Sweet Stuff, which is only the very best candy store in Riverhurst. Uncle Nick bought us a big bag of chocolate-covered almonds, and a bar of Rocky Road for himself. Then we strolled around the mall, munching on chocolate and looking in windows.

The kittens in Pets of Distinction were taking turns being King of the Hill on top of their scratching post. We watched them wrestle and tumble for a few minutes. After that we browsed through Romano's, this enormous store that sells everything from lip gloss to lawn chairs. Then we bought the latest issue of *Star Turns* at Fred's Magazines and stepped into the Record Emporium just long enough to hear one cut from Heat's latest album.

Stephanie was starting to get antsy. "We've wandered around long enough, don't you think?" she whispered. "Let's just *do* it!"

"We don't want Uncle Nick to get suspicious," Patti whispered back.

We made one more stop, into Feathers and Fins, to look at the creepy-crawlies. Horace has a whole collection of slimers in the Jenkinses' basement — lizards, turtles, a salamander. . . . So Uncle Nick bought him an assortment of dried bugs for them — flies, pieces of cricket and grasshopper. Totally gruesome! The salesman shoveled the bugs into a little white carton with a wire handle, like the ones they pack fried rice into for Chinese take-out, and handed it to Uncle Nick.

Finally we headed up the center aisle of the mall again, toward Just Juniors — and Lucy Wilder!

We usually stop outside the store at least long enough to check out everything that's new in the window. But that afternoon we pushed open the glass door as soon as we got there.

"I'll wait for you," Uncle Nick said, about to sit

down on a bench in the center aisle.

"Oh, please come with us," Patti pleaded.

"Sometimes we need a man's opinion," Stephanie added seriously.

Kate rolled her eyes. I could tell she thought Stephanie was going a little too far, but I poked her with my elbow. After all, it was for a good cause, wasn't it?

So all five of us walked into Just Juniors. Patti, Stephanie, Kate, and I had a moment of panic when we saw Kim, one of the regular saleswomen, behind the counter, and nobody else.

"Maybe Lucy took Saturday off," Kate muttered.

But then she appeared in the door of the storeroom!

"Hey, girls!" Lucy called out over the music. "I have some fantastic new jumpsuits that just came in. Want to see them?"

Lucy was wearing bright green leggings and a red-and-green crop top. Her lip color, according to Stephanie, was Cinnamon Dreams. She'd crimped her blonde hair. She looked *supremo*!

"Sure!" we said.

Then Lucy noticed Uncle Nick, hanging out near the front of the store. She kind of sized him up, and glanced over at us, and back at him, as if to say,

"Does this cute guy belong to you?" Our plan was working!

.I couldn't tell if Uncle Nick focused on Lucy at all, though, until Patti introduced them. "Lucy, this is my uncle, Nick Pollard. Uncle Nick, this is Lucy Wilder."

Lucy smiled and stuck out her hand, and Uncle Nick set the container of dried bugs down on the counter and stretched out his hand. "Hello."

"Have you moved to Riverhurst? Or are you just visiting?" Lucy asked him.

"I'm on my vacation," Uncle Nick said. Now he was smiling, too.

"So the girls are showing you around the mall? They're the best guides you could want. I can't think of anyone who knows it better than they do," Lucy said. That's probably true. Most Saturdays, we practically *live* at the mall.

"Where have you taken Nick?" Lucy wanted to know. "The Pizza Palace? Romano's?"

Stephanie nodded. "Yes, and Pets of Distinction, and Sweet Stuff. . . ."

"Is that what you have in the bag?" Lucy said. "Chocolates?"

"Want some?" Patti asked, holding out the chocolate-covered almonds.

"No, thanks. I'll try one of Nick's," Lucy said, looking up at Uncle Nick with a big smile.

Before we realized what she was talking about, Lucy Wilder pulled open the top of the little white container from Feathers and Fins and reached into it!

"No!" Stephanie shouted.

"Stop!" Kate yelled.

"Those are — " Patti and I began.

But Lucy drowned us all out with a totally disgusted *shriek*! and dropped the whole box on the polished wood floor!

Needless to say, we never got to look at the fantastic new jumpsuits. Once we'd swept up the flies and dried cricket parts, we headed for home.

"I don't think Lucy Wilder even looked at Uncle Nick again," I whispered to Stephanie. She, Kate, and I were sitting in the second seat of the van.

"It was kind of funny, though," Kate murmured. "There was Lucy Wilder dressed to the teeth and sort of interested in the guy. And she sticks her hand into a container full of *bugs*!" We tried not to giggle, because unfortunately Uncle Nick seemed even gloomier than he had been that morning. So much for our great plan. . . .

He dropped Kate off at her house first. Then just

before Uncle Nick pulled into my driveway, Stephanie murmured in my ear, "It's back to the old drawing board. And I mean the *drawing* board. It's Ms. Gilberto's turn next."

But something happened on Monday that made us forget all about Uncle Nick and his problems. At least for a while.

Chapter
5

Kate, Patti, Stephanie, and I met at the corner of Pine and Hillcrest on Monday morning, as usual. And we rode our bikes to school together, as usual. And we slid into our desks in 5B at about eight thirty-seven, as usual. But that was just about the last usual thing that happened all day.

Because the person sitting at the front of the room wasn't our teacher, Mrs. Mead. It was Mrs. Wainwright, the Riverhurst Elementary School principal! The kids who were already in class were dead quiet, even though the final bell hadn't rung yet.

"Henry Larkin must have done something *major* this time," Kate wrote on the back of her math notebook. Henry Larkin's a guy in our class who goofs off a lot. But everybody really likes him. I think some

43

people really *really* like him. In fact, there's a question I have for Patti about Henry, the next time we play Truth or Dare. . . .

Mrs. Wainwright rapped on Mrs. Mead's desk with her knuckles, as she cleared her throat. "Since you all seem to be here, class. . . ." She paused. Mrs. Wainwright is a small woman with silvery-gray hair, and pale blue eyes. Henry claims one look from those eyes can turn anyone to stone. All I know is, you could have heard a pin drop in 5B that morning.

Mrs. Wainwright went on, "I wanted to tell you personally about Mrs. Mead."

Almost all the kids gasped! Had something awful happened to our teacher?!

But Mrs. Wainwright was shaking her head. "Mrs. Mead is *all right*. But she did have to have emergency surgery to remove her appendix on Sunday. And I'm afraid she'll be at home, recovering, for the next couple of weeks. You will have a substitute teacher during that time, a Ms. . . . ah . . . here she is!"

Mrs. Wainwright turned toward the door, and her secretary, Mrs. Jamison, ushered in a very pretty young woman with reddish-brown hair in a French braid.

"Allll ri-i-ight!" I heard Mark Freedman mutter behind me. In fact, all the boys in class suddenly sat up straighter in their seats.

"This is Ms. Chipley, children," Mrs. Wainwright said. "She is an excellent teacher, with many interesting things to share with you. I'm counting on all of you to make her stay at Riverhurst Elementary both pleasant and rewarding." No matter how Mrs. Wainwright starts out, she always ends up sounding as though she's giving a speech in the auditorium.

"Now, let's welcome Ms. Chipley with a big round of applause," Mrs. Wainwright ordered.

Everybody clapped politely, and Ms. Chipley gave us a quick smile in return. Then she walked Mrs. Wainwright and Mrs. Jamison to the door, where they talked in low voices for a couple of minutes.

Stephanie hurriedly dropped a note on the floor in front of me — she sits in the first row, and Kate and I sit in the second, right behind her: *A great — underlined three times — outfit!*

I had to admit, Ms. Chipley's sky-blue silk shirt, gray-and-cream pleated pants, and American Indian concho belt and turquoise earrings were a little snappier than Mrs. Mead's dark colored skirts and sweaters. Maybe two weeks without our regular teacher would be okay. It might even be fun! After all, Mrs. Mead *does* give a lot of homework.

Ms. Chipley closed the door behind Mrs. Wainwright and Mrs. Jamison. She stepped over to the blackboard and wrote her name: C-H-I-P-L-E-Y. Then she turned around to face the class. Everyone settled back comfortably, expecting at least twenty minutes of introducing *our*selves. But the first words out of Ms. Chipley's mouth were, "Please take out a pencil and paper for a math quiz."

When some of the kids groaned, she cut them off, fast, with, "I'll be glad to deal with any complaints after three o'clock. Or you may discuss them with the principal immediately."

So the old Chipper (which was what Henry nicknamed her *right away*) got down to business, and a school day has never seemed so long! The math quiz was only the beginning. Instead of just discussion, like we have with Mrs. Mead, we had questions and answers about the circulatory system during science, which was awful for everybody. The kids who hadn't studied it the night before were embarrassed because they sounded dumb — like Larry Jackson, for example.

When Ms. Chipley pointed to Larry and asked, "What are the four main blood groups?", he answered, "A . . . B . . . uh . . . C, and D!"

"I want the blood groups, *not* the alphabet," Ms. Chipley replied sharply.

Henry and Pete Stone got it wrong, too, until finally Robin Becker said, "A, B, AB, and O."

But the kids who got the answers right were embarrassed, too, because *they* sounded like they were showing off. All except Karla Stamos, of course. Karla's the class grind. She studies all the time, which is fine, but she loves showing off what she knows. She's always giving people study tips they don't want, or bragging about how smart she is, even though Patti's about ten times smarter. Karla actually seemed to *like* Ms. Chipley, grinning and nodding at everything she said.

During reading, Ms. Chipley ordered Henry Larkin to Mrs. Wainwright's office for flipping a rubber band at Angela Kemp.

"But I didn't mean to — my finger slipped!" Henry protested.

"Are you arguing with me?" Ms. Chipley said sternly.

And Henry was history for the rest of the morning.

As Patti said during lunch, "Mrs. Mead would *never* have done that. She would have made a little joke about Henry's twitchy trigger finger, or something, and asked him to write her a paragraph about acting up in class. And we would have gone ahead with reading. I think Ms. Chipley totally overreacted!"

"Totally!" Stephanie said. "If one rubber band lands you in the principal's office, what happens if you're late? You get sent to jail?!" Kate and I couldn't have agreed more!

That afternoon, Ms. Chipley assigned a book report for Friday and handed out a long list of words for a spelling quiz the next day. For social studies, she wanted a one-page paper on current events in Canada, to be turned in the first thing the next morning! When the bell rang at three o'clock, we staggered out of 5B more dead than alive, and it was only Monday.

Mark, Larry Jackson, and Henry were hanging around the bike rack, griping. "Got to hand it to the old Chipper," Mark said. "She makes Mrs. Mead look like the easiest teacher in the world."

"If she's this bad the first day, what's she going to do for an encore?" Henry said. Then he added gloomily, "I'm sure *I'll* be the very first to find out!"

"Kar-la thinks she's suuu-per!" Larry Jackson did an imitation of Karla Stamos's scratchy voice and pointed to the building behind us. "Look at Karla, buttering the old Chipper up!"

"Give me a break!" Henry muttered.

Ms. Chipley and Karla were walking down the front steps of the school. Karla was chattering away noisily, and Ms. Chipley was nodding and putting in a word here and there.

"They might as well hang around together. Nobody else will get near either of them," Mark said, holding his nose. "You guys want to ride with us to Charlie's?" Charlie's Soda Fountain is on Main Street, only a few blocks from Riverhurst Elementary.

"Yeah, come on. We're going to drown our troubles in some super-deluxe Coke floats," Henry said, poking Patti's arm. Henry used to be one of the shorter boys in fourth grade, but he's grown a lot this year. Now, he's almost as tall as Patti is.

"I can't. I have chores to do at home," I said. My mom has started working again, and I help out by doing some of the washing and vacuuming.

"I'm going home, too," Kate said. "It'll take me *hours* to slog through all this homework, and I really want to watch an old movie on Channel 24 tonight."

"I promised my Uncle Nick that we'd do the grocery shopping together," Patti said. "I thought I might be able to keep him out of trouble," she added to us in a lower voice.

"Then we'll see you around." Mark, Larry, and Henry jumped on their bikes and coasted down Hillcrest.

"Wow! The Chipper pushed Uncle Nick completely out of my mind!" Stephanie said, unlocking her bike. "And Ms. Gilberto! How could I have forgotten the match of the century?!"

"Do you have a plan yet?" I asked her.

"I'll think of one tonight," Stephanie said. "In between social studies and spelling!"

"Check out Karla," Kate murmured as we pulled our bikes out of the rack.

Karla was holding Ms. Chipley's books while the Chipper opened the back of a little blue car parked at the curb. Farther down the sidewalk, a group of girls from our class — Jane Sykes, Robin Becker, Sally Mason, Erin Wilson — were staring at them and whispering. As we rode by, Erin pointed at Karla and made a face. Erin's pretty nice and doesn't usually give anyone a hard time. But acting all buddy-buddy with the Chipper wasn't exactly the best way to win friends. . . .

"Karla must really enjoy being unpopular," Stephanie said as we headed up Hillcrest. "Getting on Chipley's good side is the kiss of death!"

My thoughts exactly!

Chapter
6

By Tuesday morning, we were even more bummed out about our substitute teacher, if that was possible.

"It took me two hours just to do the social studies paper!" Kate fumed as we waited for Patti to show up at the corner. "I missed the first twenty minutes of *Slim Malone*. It's a classic — filmed *on location* in Africa in 1934. And because I didn't see the beginning I never figured out the plot!"

"I dreamed about the spelling list in my sleep!" Stephanie complained. "And I was all set to dream about Kevin DeSpain!" Kevin DeSpain's the hunk on *Made for Each Other* on Channel 6. We actually *met* him when he came to Riverhurst to film an episode at Chesterfield, this big old estate up the river. "I stared really hard at his poster just before I closed my eyes . . . but what did I dream about instead? *Retrieve* and *wrought!*" Stephanie looked totally disgusted.

"I started reading the book, *How Our Economy Works*, for the book report on Friday," I told them. "I couldn't believe how boring it was. The first fifteen pages were nothing but blah, blah, blah. I don't think Ms. Chipley has a clue about what kids like."

"I don't think she has a clue about what kids *are* like," Kate said wisely.

Then Patti whizzed up to us on her bike. "Hey, guys!"

"Hi, Patti! What's new with Uncle Nick?" Stephanie asked.

Patti shook her head. "Not good. He was so out of it yesterday that he wandered into the edge of one of those pyramids of cans at Save-Mart. Cans of pork-and-beans rolled everywhere! There must have been at least five stock boys scrambling around after them on their hands and knees."

"Oh, no!" But we had to laugh.

"Uncle Nick really is a walking disaster," Kate said.

"Don't worry about it. I have a plan to get Uncle Nick and Ms. Gilberto together," Stephanie announced. "It's simple, but brilliant."

"Not one of those!" Kate groaned as we pedaled down Hillcrest toward school. "It was one of your simple plans that wrecked Lauren's yard and got her grounded for weeks!" Stephanie had decided to become famous by joining a rock band, but the only way the sixth-grade guitarist would let her join was if she found the group a place to practice. Stephanie figured, with my mom away at work as well as my dad, our garage would be perfect. . . .

"It's nothing like that," Stephanie said quickly when I frowned at her suspiciously. "We'll just invite Uncle Nick to look at the mural at the new studio! It's been written up in the paper as one of the must-see sights in Riverhurst. And *we're* in it!"

A few months ago, Ms. Gilberto and her art classes at Riverhurst Elementary moved from the old studio, in the basement of the school, to a brand-new studio on the other side of the auditorium. It's big and airy, and has lots of light.

The outside walls are decorated with scenes of the school. The best fourth-, fifth-, and sixth-grade artists painted kids studying, in the library, in the gym, playing baseball, and just hanging out. And Stephanie painted the Sleepover Friends, at our regular table in the cafeteria! One of Kate's eyebrows is raised, Patti's smiling, and Stephanie and I are laughing our heads off. It's the Sleepover Friends, forever! Or at least until the art studio crumbles to dust.

"What good will it do for Uncle Nick to see the mural?" Kate said. "He can't visit during school hours, and Ms. Gilberto leaves at three."

"Not this Thursday. A bunch of us are going to stay after school and do silk-screening with her," Stephanie informed us. "Patti can bring him over then!"

"I'll try," Patti said. She didn't sound very hopeful. "But I have a feeling Uncle Nick realized we were up to something at Just Juniors on Saturday."

Our bikes bumped to a stop against the curb in front of the school. Kate checked her watch. "Eight thirty-six," she said. All the kids were starting to file into the building, because the first bell had already rung.

"We'd better hustle," Stephanie said. "I think the best way to survive the Chipper is to blend into the woodwork, and not give her an excuse to single us out. She doesn't know who anybody is yet, so let's keep it that way."

I agreed. Acting like Pete Stone, who howled when he got his math test back, was definitely a bad idea. (I could see his grade, on the upper right-hand corner of the paper, from my desk — a big, fat D.) Ms. Chipley watched him for the rest of the morning like a hawk ready to swoop.

Kate, Stephanie, Patti, and I got through math all right — I ended up with a B on my test. And luckily the four of us had studied more about circulation, because, sure enough, there was another question-and-answer session about it. My questions were easy: "What's the largest blood vessel in the body?" The aorta. And "What are leucocytes?" I might not know how to spell the word, but I knew what it meant: white blood cells. I'd decided it was a little better to look smart and have some of the kids roll their eyes at me, than look dumb and get the Chipper on my case!

Reading was no sweat, either. It was after lunch that the trouble started, and in a way that we never could have imagined in a million years.

Ms. Chipley clapped her hands together for attention, although nobody was talking — nobody dared. "Class," she said, "I'll be handing back the social studies papers on Canadian current events."

Kate raised an eyebrow at me, meaning, *"Already?!"* I mean, we'd only turned them in that morning! I guess Ms. Chipley would rather grade papers than eat lunch. She was a regular teaching machine!

"But before I do that, I'd like to say something about one of the papers. . . ."

"Uh-oh," I was thinking. "I *knew* I should have borrowed Roger's typewriter. Now she's going to make an example of my handwriting!" I've got awfully messy handwriting, and the night before I'd made a hole in the paper trying to neaten up.

But Miss Chipley went on, " . . . actually, about one of the *students*. There's a girl in this class . . ."

A girl! I saw Larry Jackson give a sigh of relief. But wait — Ms. Chipley wasn't upset at anybody, after all, because she continued, " . . . a girl who has written an excellent paper, so good that I'd like to share it with you."

Karla Stamos started grinning like a jack-o'-lantern, certain that Ms. Chipley was talking about her. But her face fell when the Chipper added, "Not only is her social studies paper exceptional, but she earned an A on the math quiz as well." Karla's not so great at math.

Ms. Chipley held up Mrs. Mead's black gradebook. "Since I haven't begun to match many of these names to your faces yet, perhaps she won't mind raising her hand . . . Patti Jenkins!"

Poor Patti! Talk about being singled out! Her face faded to white, and then blushed dark red. She really didn't want to raise her hand at all. But she sits in the corner in the last row in 5B, and when Ms. Chipley announced her name, every kid in the class swiveled around to stare at her. Patti looked ready to drop through the floor, or maybe climb out a window. But it wasn't hard to figure out where everybody was peering, so Ms. Chipley positively beamed at Patti. And Patti finally raised her hand in a shaky kind of way.

"Congratulations!" Ms. Chipley burbled. "You have written a very well-organized paper that's informative and entertaining." With every word Patti seemed to sink lower in her seat. "I didn't have a single suggestion to make about it!" Ms. Chipley went on. "It was absolutely perfect." She just wouldn't leave off.

Then she started to read Patti's paper, "Canada: Boom or Bust," out loud. But I don't think I heard a single word. I felt too terrible for Patti. I knew she must be absolutely dying!

I noticed Jenny Carlin and her best friend, Angela Kemp, smirking at each other. David Degan was gazing at the ceiling as though he was ready to pass out from boredom. And Karla Stamos was making a big show of twiddling her thumbs.

They were all jealous, of course, and it made me mad. Patti's the type of person who has plenty to brag about, but never opens her mouth. I glared at Jenny and Angela. It just wasn't fair!

Not everybody was being nasty. Mark and Henry were acting perfectly normal, staring straight ahead while they stepped on each other's sneakers. Sally Mason was sketching in her notebook, and Robin Becker was writing a name over and over again, but I couldn't tell from where I was sitting whether it was "Tommy," or "Todd."

Finally, after what felt like *hours*, Ms. Chipley's mouth stopped moving. She beamed at the back of the room again, but I didn't dare turn around to find out what kind of shape Patti was in.

And Ms. Chipley still wasn't through with her. She went on to say she'd noticed in the grade book that all of Patti's grades were superior, and that Patti was obviously good at everything she put her mind to.

"Patti Jenkins is a model student," Ms. Chipley added, in case we'd missed the point. "It wouldn't hurt the rest of you to try to be a little more like her."

Jenny made a face at Angela. David Degan didn't stop staring at the ceiling, and Karla Stamos glared in Patti's direction. Bummer!

What had Stephanie said? "Getting on Chipley's good side is the kiss of death!"

Luckily we had the spelling test to get through, which took Ms. Chipley's mind off Patti. And when school was over, Patti shot out of the classroom like a rocket! I think Ms. Chipley had intended to say something more to Patti privately, but she didn't get the chance — as soon as the last bell rang, Patti was gone!

Chapter
7

Patti was awfully quiet during the bike ride home. Stephanie, Kate, and I gabbed away to fill the empty spaces, but nothing we said seemed to cheer Patti up. Patti didn't have much to say the next morning, either. But she *did* have a bandage on her left index finger.

"What happened?" Stephanie asked her as we rolled down the hill toward school.

Patti shrugged, her eyes on the road. I imagined she was wondering what Ms. Chipley had in store for her *that* day. Finally she said in an embarrassed voice, "I slammed a drawer on it by accident."

"Science isn't the only thing that runs in her family," Kate murmured to me.

We were a little earlier than usual when we rode

up to the bike rack. Larry Jackson and Henry Larkin shouted from the side steps, "Hey — come talk to us!"

Kate and Stephanie started toward them. But Patti walked over to the little kids' swings and sat down on one. I followed her and squeezed into another.

"Look, Patti — everybody already knows you're smart, with the Quarks and everything," I began cautiously. "They don't hold it against you. And Ms. Chipley's only here for eight more days. . . ."

"If she keeps this up for *eight days*, I'll be about as popular as Karla Stamos!" Patti said fiercely. "But she's not going to keep it up."

"She's not? What are you going to do?" I wanted to know. I mean, Stephanie's usually the one who makes *plans*.

"You'll see," Patti said, nodding her head firmly.

I wasn't sure Patti was going to manage to do anything. She stumbled going up the front steps, tripped over her shoelaces, and almost crashed into Miss Rosen in the hall. But as soon as we got to class I *saw*, all right!

When we stepped into 5B, Ms. Chipley gave Patti a big, friendly, "Hello!" But Patti barely nodded in return. She walked silently past the teacher's desk, not looking either left or right, to her seat in the back of the room. Ms. Chipley stared after her with a puzzled expression.

Stephanie nudged me with her elbow on her way to her own desk and whispered, hardly moving her lips, "What gives?" Kate raised *both* eyebrows as high as they would go. But Patti was just getting started!

The late bell rang, and math class began. Ms. Chipley opened Mrs. Mead's grade book and picked the names of four kids to work out some of the homework problems on the blackboard. Patti was one of the kids she called on.

Patti strolled slowly up to the board, carefully picked up a piece of chalk, and proceeded to do the problem *wrong*! I couldn't believe it, and neither could anybody else in the room.

Jenny leaned over to whisper something in Angela's ear, and they both snickered. Karla smiled one of her most self-satisfied smiles. David Degan peered at Patti's answer and smirked importantly.

Mark Freedman, who was standing next to Patti at the board, muttered the right answer to her under his breath. But Patti acted as if she hadn't heard. She left it the way she'd done it!

Ms. Chipley went down the line of kids at the board, checking their answers: "Good . . . well done . . . good work . . ." Then she came to Patti's answer. Ms. Chipley looked at it and frowned. She tilted her reddish-brown head and waited, giving Patti a chance to fix her mistakes, but Patti stood her ground.

"Can anyone tell me the correct answer to this problem?" Ms. Chipley asked the other kids in the class.

Karla Stamos waved her hand in the air so hard that her arm looked ready to drop off at the shoulder. She was probably remembering the A Patti had made on her math quiz on Monday, and was thrilled to have a chance to show her up. Finally Ms. Chipley put Karla out of her misery by calling on her. "Karla?"

"Four-hundred-and-six-dollars-and-forty-eight-cents!" Karla said in a rush.

"That's right, Karla," said Ms. Chipley approvingly. "Would you like to come to the board and show us how you got your answer?"

Would she *like* to! Wild animals couldn't have kept her away! Karla pranced up to the board, and Patti walked back to her desk in defeat. But she certainly didn't *look* defeated. . . .

In science Patti couldn't seem to remember the

simplest facts about circulation, like whether the veins pump blood *to* or *from* the heart, or exactly why the aorta's important, or what capillaries are. And during reading she read "though" for "thought," and "nice" for "niece." It was incredible!

But Ms. Chipley bought it! By the time the lunch bell rang, she was definitely starting to look worried.

She wasn't the only one. As soon as we'd filed down the hall to the cafeteria, Stephanie asked anxiously, "Patti, are you all right?"

"Maybe you're coming down with the flu," Kate said. She looked practically ready to take Patti's temperature right there in the lunch line. "It's going around."

"She's doing it on purpose!" I said crossly, because I couldn't help thinking Patti was making a big mistake. "Aren't you?!"

Patti didn't say yes, but she didn't say no, either, and her cheeks turned bright pink.

"You're kidding!" Stephanie exclaimed, gawking at her. "You're faking all this?!"

I nodded. "Because of the Chipper."

"Just how long do you intend to keep this up?" Kate asked Patti sternly.

But right then Henry Larkin interrupted, leaning

in front of us to grab a carton of milk. "Don't let it get you down," he told Patti. "Nobody can be right all the time."

"Except Karla," Mark Freedman cut in. "And look at *her*." Mark wiggled his thumb toward the far end of the cafeteria, where Karla was sitting at a table all by herself. "She'd have to *pay* somebody to sit with her."

"Anyway, don't worry about your slump. Everyone strikes out once in a while," Henry said, and smiled. He has a great smile — there's a tiny space between his two front teeth that's actually kind of cute. "You'll snap out of it. You'll be batting a thousand again before you know it."

Then he and Mark waved and headed for a corner table, where Larry was already scarfing down his meatloaf on a roll. When they were gone, Kate turned to Patti and said, "And just when *do* you plan to snap out of this slump?"

"Seven and a half more days," Patti replied apologetically.

Kate shook her head. "I think that's crazy!" she said. I had to agree. But Patti was determined.

By the time Patti had fumbled her way through the Wednesday afternoon classes, though, even Ms.

66

Chipley had had enough. Just as the three o'clock bell rang she announced, "I'd like to see Patti Jenkins, please. The rest of you may go."

Several of the kids gave Patti pitying looks. Henry made the thumbs-up sign.

"We'll meet you on the front steps," I mouthed to her. Then Kate, Stephanie, and I followed the crowd out of 5B.

We hadn't been waiting too long when Patti appeared. She was sort of red-faced, but she held her head high.

"What did the Chipper say?" Stephanie asked excitedly as soon as we'd moved out of earshot of the school building.

"Not much," Patti replied. "She wanted to know if I was having any problems I wanted to talk about."

"Yes, Ms. Chipley — you!" I answered for her.

Patti grinned wanly. "Exactly. And when I couldn't come up with any, she started to get upset. She kept asking me if I was sure. And when I said, 'Yes,' she pulled a piece of paper off a notepad, scribbled something on it, stuffed it into a little envelope, and told me to give it to my parents!"

Patti reached into her jacket pocket and took out a small white envelope.

"Uh-oh. I got one of those in third grade, from Mrs. Peters," I said, shaking my head.

"For what?" Stephanie asked.

"For punching Wayne Miller in the nose!" Kate answered, grinning.

I really did! And to this day, I'm not sorry. Wayne Miller is still the meanest boy in school!

"Did you tell Ms. Chipley your parents are away?" Kate said.

Patti shook her head. "No — Uncle Nick can read the note," she answered.

"Are you going to stop pretending you're dumb now?" Stephanie asked.

"In seven more days," Patti replied stubbornly.

Chapter
8

Fate sometimes has a way of punching you in the nose to get your attention, sort of like I punched Wayne Miller. And it did just that to Patti the very next day.

She told us what Ms. Chipley had written in the note. "Uncle Nick showed it to me," she said as we talked on the corner of Hillcrest and Pine. " 'Dear Mr. and Mrs. Jenkins, I am a little concerned about the rapid deterioration in quality — ' " Patti quoted from memory.

"Deterioration?" I interrupted. "What does that mean?"

"It means falling apart — I looked it up," Patti said. " . . . 'in the quality of your daughter Patti's performance in my class. I would like very much to meet with you as soon as possible to discuss the problem. I have set aside a time to see one or both of you at three forty-five tomorrow — Thursday — afternoon in 5B. However, if you would like to reschedule, please call Mrs. Jamison at the school office to set up another appointment. Yours sincerely, Tara Chipley.' "

"Tara?" Kate sniffed.

"Ta-ra, ta-ra!" Stephanie made a noise like a trumpet. "Tara the Terrible!"

"Was Uncle Nick mad?" I asked.

"No. When he showed me the note, he seemed more . . . *surprised,*" Patti said.

"So, is he meeting the Chipper today?" Stephanie asked. And when Patti nodded, she went on, "I guess Ms. Gilberto is on hold, then."

"Yeah," Patti said glumly. "I guess so — unfortunately." She sighed. "But Uncle Nick sure isn't getting any better on his own."

"Did he break anything last night?" I wanted to know.

"Only the table," said Patti.

"The table?" Stephanie and I squawked.

But before Patti could tell us *how,* Kate exclaimed, "Listen guys, we better step on it. It's already eight thirty-five!"

We raced down Hillcrest and skidded to a stop at the bike rack. We were locking up our bikes when somebody yelled, "Hey, Patti!" Two sixth-grade girls, Lindsay Vlasak and Harriet Mills, came running over to us.

"We've been waiting for you!" Lindsay said breathlessly. She's short, with curly brown hair and braces.

"Bill Bertolas is sick!" Harriet added. Harriet's about Patti's size and has bright red hair and freckles. "He caught chicken pox from his little brother. He'll be in bed for *weeks!*"

"Oh?" Patti was wondering what that had to do with her, and so were the rest of us.

"So we want *you!*" Harriet said.

Patti looked puzzled.

"We want you to replace him on the Science Bowl!" Lindsay explained. "Mr. Murdock" — he's one of the sponsors of the Quarks club, and a graduate student in biology at the university — "and Mrs. Wainwright have already talked it over."

"Me?" Patti squeaked. "But why not Dana Rice? Or Elizabeth Chan?" They're both sixth-graders.

"Dana freezes in front of an audience," Harriet replied. "And Elizabeth is sick, too, with the flu. Besides, Mrs. Wainwright decided it would be nice to have a fifth-grader on the team. And nobody could do a better job than you, Patti."

Patti looked down at her feet. Kate, Stephanie, and I exchanged glances. Even in her dumb phase?

"But what about Betsy Chalfin? Or Todd Farrell?" Patti mumbled more names. She suddenly looked sort of sick herself.

"None of them are any good in front of a crowd, either," Harriet said firmly.

"A crowd?" Kate repeated. "I thought the contest was going to be in the auditorium during school hours."

"Right — at ten o'clock, but the whole school will be dismissed to see it," Lindsay said. "Plus anybody else who wants to come."

"There'll be a big audience, because Dr. Know will be asking the questions!" Harriet added excitedly.

"Dr. Know from the *Dr. Know Show*?" Stephanie exclaimed. "Since when?"

"Since yesterday," Harriet said. "He's going to bring a camera crew to videotape it, to use on his new series!"

The late bell rang, and I jumped a mile!

"We're doomed!" Stephanie wailed. "The

Chipper will be standing at the door with handcuffs!''

"Talk to you at lunch!" Harriet shouted at our retreating backs.

"Yeah, sure. We'll be spending lunch with Mrs. Wainwright!" Kate moaned, as we clattered up the sidewalk. If you're late more than once at Riverhurst Elementary, you have to spend your lunch hour with the principal. That's an experience I've already had twice, thank you, and I don't care to repeat it.

But Ms. Chipley completely ignored the four of us as we tiptoed hurriedly to our seats. She just went on with the math lesson as if nothing had happened. She must have decided on a new approach with Patti, which was very lucky for Stephanie, Kate, and me!

That morning Patti wouldn't have had to *fake* being dumb. She was so flipped out about the Science Bowl that she probably couldn't have remembered her own name! But the Chipper didn't call on her, not once. In fact, I couldn't help noticing that the dreadful Ms. Chipley was lightening up a little. Maybe teaching 5B was showing her a thing or two about kids. . . .

When lunchtime came, Patti dragged us aside on our way to the cafeteria. *"I can't do it,"* she said. "I just can't! Being Chipley's pet-for-a-day was bad

73

enough. But being on the Science Bowl in front of the whole world?! The kids will banish me to permanent geekdom!"

"No, they won't. They'll be proud of you!" Kate said sensibly. "Come on, Patti. It's for the school! Like winning the soccer league play-offs!"

"Or beating Dannerville in a baseball game!" I told her, remembering Henry's talk about a batting slump.

Which was more or less Harriet and Lindsay's argument. They pounced on us the second we sat down at our regular table with our Thursday lunch: macaroni and cheese, carrot sticks, and chilled fruit. As soon as they opened their mouths it was clear they meant business.

"If you won't do it, we'll have to stand up in front of the whole school . . ." Lindsay began.

"And Dr. Know's television audience," Harriet went on, "and *forfeit!*"

"Forfeit?" Stephanie said.

"Right — say we officially withdraw from the contest," Lindsay told her. She made it sound like the worst!

"Quit before we even get started," Harriet added. "The Riverhurst Quitters!"

"Patti!" said Kate — Kate's never quit *anything*!

"Patti?" I said.

"Come on, Patti," Stephanie said. "For the school! Do you want Dannerville to think we're chicken?"

"Or those wise-guys in Hampton to beat us?" Kate asked.

Patti looked completely miserable. I guess she figured she'd lose, either way. If she *didn't* do it, she'd be letting down the Quarks and the whole school. And if she *did* do it . . .

Finally Patti nodded her head, and said in a very weak voice, "Okay . . . count me in."

"Terrific!" Lindsay exclaimed.

"You won't be sorry!" said Harriet, squeezing her arm.

"I'm sorry already," Patti murmured, watching Henry Larkin and Mark Freedman and Larry Jackson clowning around on the other side of the cafeteria.

Chapter
9

Patti was in a trance for the rest of the afternoon. She still sounded kind of out of it when I spoke to her on the telephone that evening. I'd called to find out about Uncle Nick's meeting with the Chipper.

"He didn't say much," Patti told me, "except he was sure we could work it out, whatever *that* means. And he hasn't broken anything since he got home, but he *has* been whistling a lot. . . ."

Whistling? Ms. Chipley didn't make me nervous enough to whistle, but she did make me want to scream!

At ten o'clock on Friday morning, a new bell rang, the bell for the Science Bowl. All the kids in

Riverhurst Elementary filed out of their classrooms and clumped down the hall toward the auditorium. Except for Patti, Harriet, and Lindsay, that is — they'd been huddled in the empty cafeteria with Mr. Murdock since eight o'clock going over questions that might be asked in the contest.

"There's Uncle Nick!" Kate said as we followed Ms. Chipley through the auditorium doors and up the aisle between folding chairs. Uncle Nick was sitting on the right, along with a bunch of parents and teachers. He was wearing his blue tweed sweater — the one that brings out the color of his eyes.

"Who's he waving at?" Stephanie hissed over her shoulder.

Someone ahead of us . . . I peered around kids toward the front of our line just in time to see Ms. Chipley waving back with a big smile on her face. "The Chipper!" I gasped.

"Sssh!" Karla Stamos, who was a few steps behind us, shushed me.

Five B turned to the left. All the kids sat down with a clatter, and began to cough and fidget, and stare up at the empty stage. There were three groups of three school desks onstage, arranged in a half circle around a large table. "That must be where Dr. Know will sit," Kate murmured to me about the table.

"Uncle Nick won't be able to turn down the sound on Dr. Know this time," Stephanie whispered, and all of us started to giggle.

As soon as the last class was seated, Mrs. Wainwright stepped out onto the stage and spoke into the microphone. "Good morning, students and guests. We're proud here at Riverhurst Elementary to be hosting the Science Bowl, a contest between some of our outstanding science students, and those at Dannerville and Hampton Elementary Schools. For those of you not familiar with this yearly event, each of the students has a small bell on his or her desk." Mrs. Wainwright pointed them out. The bells were the little roundish kind that have a button to bang on top.

"Our master of ceremonies will ask a question. Then the student who rings his or her bell fastest will get a chance to answer it. If the answer is correct, that student's team earns ten points. If the answer is incorrect, a student from an opposing school has a chance at it. The team with the most points at the end of the half-hour period wins this beautiful trophy for their school." Mrs. Wainwright held up a

78

fabulous-looking gold trophy with a big sun at the top.

"But before we begin," said Mrs. Wainwright, "let me bring out a man who really needs no introduction, our wonderful master of ceremonies . . . Dr. Know!"

Dr. Know is a short, plump guy with a long nose and a bald head. He bounced onto the stage as though he had springs on his feet. "Hello, boys and girls!" he boomed into the microphone. "I'm here with my camera crew today" — he pointed to the wings, where cameras and lights were set up — "to film a re-e-eally exciting contest. So without further ado, let's meet the contestants! Starting with Riverhurst, Ms. Harriet Mills!"

Harriet stepped onto the stage, wearing a bright yellow jumpsuit and red sneakers, her red hair pinned up in coils on the sides of her head. All of us clapped loudly.

"Lindsay Vlasak!" Lindsay grinned at the audience, her braces shining. "And Patti Jenkins!" Patti squared her shoulders — she was going to make the best of it — and marched to her seat.

Next Dr. Know introduced the Hampton Team, two girls and a boy. We'd met the boy before on a class field trip to Chesterfield. His name was Jeremy

Hendricks. And last Dr. Know introduced the Dannerville kids, two boys and a girl.

"Now, do we all know how the game works?" Dr. Know asked, looking around at the three teams.

Everybody nodded.

"Then let the game begin!" Dr. Know bounced over to the table, microphone in hand, and plopped down. "First question, for ten points: How long does it take sound to travel *one* mile?"

He'd barely gotten the words out when the Dannerville girl banged her bell!

"Melissa Metcalf, from Dannerville!" said Dr. Know.

"One-fifth of a second!" said Melissa.

"I'm afraid that's incorrect. . . ."

And Harriet slammed her bell! "Five seconds!"

"Ten points to Riverhurst!" yelled Dr. Know. "What's one way to tell an alligator from a crocodile?"

Ding!

"Jeremy Hendricks?" said Dr. Know.

"When an alligator closes its mouth, no teeth stick out. When a croc closes *its* mouth, you can see side teeth in the bottom jaw!" Jeremy said.

"Absolutely right!" Dr. Know yelped.

I never thought I'd get all that excited about a

science contest, but it *was* exciting, and I learned stuff, too. Like how long a camel can go without water: over thirty days! Which mammal can squirt venom from its hind ankles? A male duck-billed platypus! And what's the tiniest bone in the human body? The stirrup bone, in your ear.

Patti answered that one and the next one: How old is the universe? About fifteen billion years old!

She was definitely on a roll, and Mark Freedman, Pete Stone, and Henry Larkin really started cheering her on.

"How long before people appeared on Earth did the dinosaurs disappear?" asked Dr. Know.

Ding! "Sixty million years!" Patti said.

And she didn't seem nervous at all!

Finally it was Riverhurst 70, and Hampton 70. Dannerville was behind with 40. There was only time for a couple more questions. . . .

"Name two of Jupiter's many moons," Dr. Know said.

Daphne Lauderbach from Hampton punched her bell. "Io . . . and Europe!" she said.

"Actually, it's Europa," said Dr. Know, "but I think we'll give you the benefit of the doubt on this one." He checked his watch. "We have time for one more question. Ready, teams?"

They were ready, and Kate, Stephanie, and I were on the edge of our chairs! If Riverhurst didn't answer this one, then Hampton had won!

"What is the most powerful muscle in the human body?" Dr. Know asked.

Ding! Lindsay Vlasak practically shrieked, "The tongue!"

"Absolutely right!" Dr. Know bounced in his seat a few times. "It's a tie game, folks. Riverhurst 80, Hampton 80! Now, the tie-breaking question in this year's Science Bowl — and it's a tough one — is . . ."

"Come on, Patti! Come on, Patti!" Stephanie, Kate, and I chanted under our breaths.

" . . . what's the name of the large white blood cells that clean up the lymph?" Dr. Know finished.

"Oh, no — a circulation question!" Kate muttered. "It's a jinx from the Chipper!"

Nobody rang a bell onstage.

"White cells that clean the lymph of dead cells and bacteria . . ." Dr. Know repeated.

Needless to say, the three of us didn't have a clue.

Patti's hand stretched out. *Di-i-ing.*

"Patti Jenkins from Riverhurst!" said Dr. Know.

"Uh . . . macrophages?" Patti said.

82

"That's it!" hollered Dr. Know. "Riverhurst wins!"

The auditorium erupted in wild applause. Dr. Know rushed over to congratulate the winning team while Harriet and Lindsay pounded Patti on her back. Our class went crazy. We jumped up and down and drummed on the floor with our feet. "Way to go!" Mark and Henry were yelling. And Ms. Chipley didn't *once* tell us to stop.

Everybody *did* have to quiet down enough for Dr. Know to present the trophy. All three teams stood up, and Dr. Know came over and stood beside them. "To the Riverhurst team, for a job very well done!" he said, handing the trophy to Harriet. Not that she'd get to keep it, of course. Once Harriet's, Lindsay's, and Patti's names had been engraved on it, it would go in the trophy case in the front hall next to Mrs. Wainwright's office.

"Do you think Patti feels funny?" Kate asked, peering up at the stage.

"It doesn't look like it," I said. Patti's face was a little pink, but she looked as pleased as I'd ever seen her. After all, she was a hero!

"Children, the lower grades may return to their classrooms," Mrs. Wainwright ordered over the microphone. "Grades four through six may remain in the auditorium for the next twenty minutes to visit with Dr. Know and the various teams."

Hampton and Dannerville hung back. The Dannerville kids looked especially disgusted with themselves — it's no fun coming in last. But Patti, Harriet, and Lindsay rushed down the stage steps into the crowd of people milling around excitedly.

"Patti — over here!" I yelled, standing on tiptoe and waving my hand in the air.

She reached us at about the same time as Uncle Nick. "You were terrific, honey!" he said, hugging her hard. "Your mom and dad are going to be so proud!"

"They have every reason to be." It was the Chipper, smiling at Patti and the three of us. "Stephanie, Kate, and Lauren, right?" I couldn't believe it — she knew our names!

Ms. Chipley smiled even wider at Uncle Nick. "You have quite a special niece, Nicholas."

"*Nicholas!*" Kate murmured.

"Wow!" said Stephanie.

"You better believe it, Tara," Uncle Nick said, with a wink at us.

"I don't think we need to look any further for someone for Uncle Nick to date," Patti whispered.

I nodded. Ms. Chipley and Uncle Nick were acting like there wasn't anyone else in the room! They kept glancing at each other and grinning. Then Ms. Chipley put her hand on Uncle Nick's arm, and leaned toward him to say something in a lower voice. "Absolutely!" we heard him murmur. "I'll pick you up around seven."

"So that's why he was whistling!" I exclaimed. "He's happy!"

"It's a good thing, too," said Stephanie. "Check out Ms. Gilberto!"

Our art teacher was standing at the front of the auditorium. She was laughing her head off with this cool-looking guy from Dr. Know's camera crew, with dark hair in a spikey haircut, and shades. He was on the stage above her, and while we were watching them, he jumped down and gave her a big kiss on the cheek!

"The secret life of Ms. Gilberto!" Stephanie said, impressed.

There was sure plenty to think about! Ms. Gilberto and the cool, dark-haired guy with the trendy haircut; Patti winning the Science Bowl; the Chipper and Uncle Nick — I hoped some of *his* teaching techniques would rub off on her, although I couldn't really imagine Ms. Chipley mixing up instant "volcanoes" during class; and the sleepover that night, at my house. . . .

Then Henry Larkin and Mark pushed through the crowd. "Hey, Patti — great save!" Henry said, smiling his cute smile. Patti blushed bright red, and Stephanie jabbed me with her elbow.

Maybe I'd make brownies after school and write "CONGRATULATIONS" on them in white icing! I couldn't wait until the sleepover . . . and that Truth or Dare game. I just had to ask Patti a question about a certain fifth-grade boy!

Sleepover Friends, forever!

SLEEPOVER FRIENDS

#23 Kate's Surprise Visitor

Denny managed to be cool for about one solid minute, chewing thoughtfully. Then I guess he couldn't stand it any longer. "Uh . . . did any of you guys happen to notice that girl?" he asked.

"Which one?" Stephanie said innocently, glancing at Kate out of the corner of her eye.

"The one in the . . . uh . . . pink and green sweater," Denny said.

"Oh, that's Michelle Olsen," Stephanie replied. "She's a seventh-grader at Riverhurst Middle School, cheerleader, beauty queen . . . ," Stephanie began to rattle off Michelle's accomplishments.

But Kate interrupted her. "Michelle's going steady!" she said firmly.

"Oh." Denny picked up his slice of double-cheese pizza and bit into it again.

Somehow I didn't really believe that was the end of it. But what happened next surprised even me.